Voting

Alan Trussell-Cullen

NELSON CENGAGE Learning

Australia • Brazil • Japan • Korea • Mexico • Singapore • Spain • United Kingdom • United States

Voting

Fast Forward
Blue Level 10

Text: Alan Trussell-Cullen
Illustrations: Boris Silvestri
Editor: Johanna Rohan
Design: Vonda Pestana
Series design: James Lowe
Production controller: Hanako Smith
Photo research: Corrina Tauschke
Audio recordings: Juliet Hill, Picture Start
Spoken by: Matthew King and Abbe Holmes
Reprint: Siew Han Ong

Acknowledgements
The author and publisher would like to acknowledge permission to reproduce material from the following sources: Photographs by AAP Image/Ben Curtis, p 15/ Alan Porritt, p 12 bottom/ Julian Smith, p 8 right; Newsphotos.com, cover, pp 1, 4, 9/Andrew Brownbill, p 10 bottom left/ Peter Kelly, p 11/ Martin Lange, p 5/ Newspix/Timothy A Clary, p 8 left; Photo Edit/Spencer Grant, back cover, pp 3, 10 top; Photolibrary.com/Photo Researchers, Inc, p 13/ Photolibrary.com/SuperStock, Inc/SuperStock, p 12 top.

Text © 2007 Alan Trussell-Cullen
Illustrations © 2007 Cengage Learning Australia Pty Limited

Copyright Notice
This Work is copyright. No part of this Work may be reproduced, stored in a retrieval system, or transmitted in any form or by any means without prior written permission of the Publisher. Except as permitted under the Copyright Act 1968, for example any fair dealing for the purposes of private study, research, criticism or review, subject to certain limitations. These limitations include: Restricting the copying to a maximum of one chapter or 10% of this book, whichever is greater; Providing an appropriate notice and warning with the copies of the Work disseminated; Taking all reasonable steps to limit access to these copies to people authorised to receive these copies; Ensuring you hold the appropriate Licences issued by the Copyright Agency Limited ("CAL"), supply a remuneration notice to CAL and pay any required fees.

ISBN 978 0 17 012543 7
ISBN 978 0 17 012537 6 (set)

Cengage Learning Australia
Level 7, 80 Dorcas Street
South Melbourne, Victoria Australia 3205
Phone: 1300 790 853

Cengage Learning New Zealand
Unit 4B Rosedale Office Park
331 Rosedale Road, Albany, North Shore NZ 0632
Phone: 0508 635 766

For learning solutions, visit cengage.com.au

Printed in China by 1010 Printing International Ltd
6 7 8 15

THE UNIVERSITY OF MELBOURNE

Evaluated in independent research by staff from the Department of Language, Literacy and Arts Education at the University of Melbourne.

Voting

Alan Trussell-Cullen

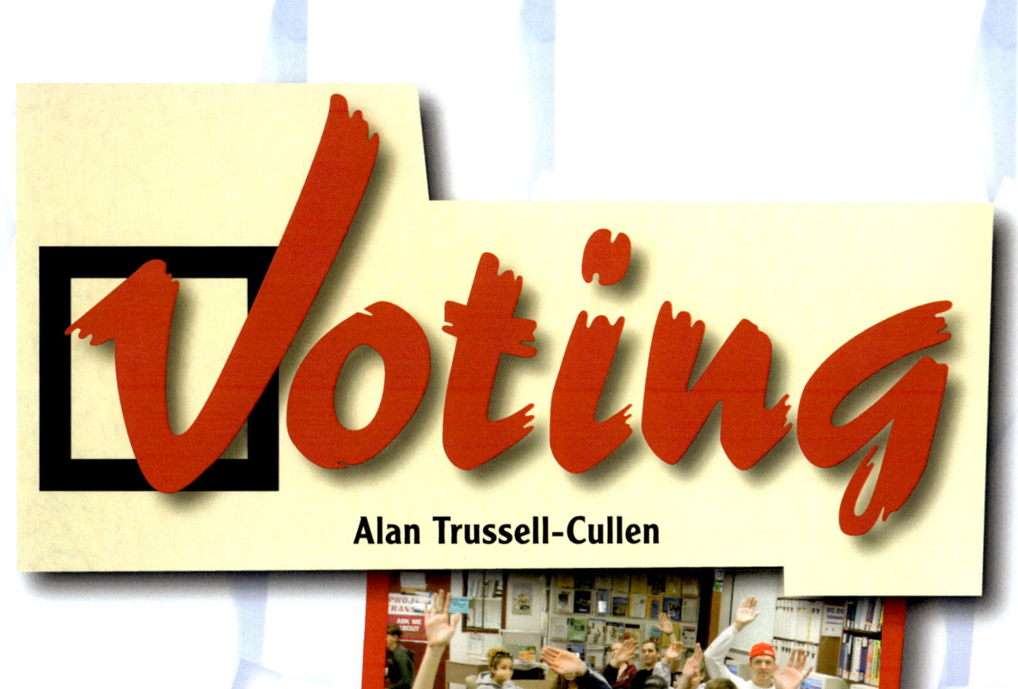

Contents

Chapter 1

WHAT IS VOTING?

Voting is when people choose something or someone they like.

Voting gives people the right to have their say.

VOTING IS VERY OLD

People have been voting for a very long time. Over 2000 years ago, the Greeks voted for the people they wanted to run their city.

They didn't always vote for the people they liked.
Sometimes, they had to vote for the people
they *didn't* want to run their city!
The person who got the most votes had to leave the city!

Chapter 3

VOTING TODAY

Today, people vote for many different things. People vote to choose someone as a leader. They vote for someone to do an important job.

Nelson Mandela

Bill Clinton

Helen Clark

Running Words 104

They vote for what they want people to do, or how they want people to do it.

They even vote for their favourite singer to win a TV competition!

Chapter 4

HOW DO PEOPLE VOTE?

There are many ways to vote. People vote by putting up their hands.

Sometimes, people don't want to tell other people who or what they voted for. It's called a **secret ballot** when people keep their vote a secret.

Paper Votes

Sometimes, people write their vote on paper. Sometimes, they choose from a list on paper.

WHAT DO YOU THINK IS BEST FOR THE CITY?

More buses? ☐

More cars? ☐

Please mark your choice with an 'x'.

Machine Votes

Sometimes, people use machines to help them vote. Machines can count the votes faster than people.

Today, people in some countries vote with computers.

Chapter 5

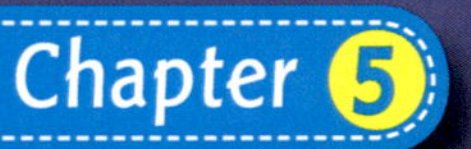

WHO VOTES?

In some countries, leaders don't always want people to vote. These leaders don't like people telling them what to do.

Some people have had to fight for the right to vote.

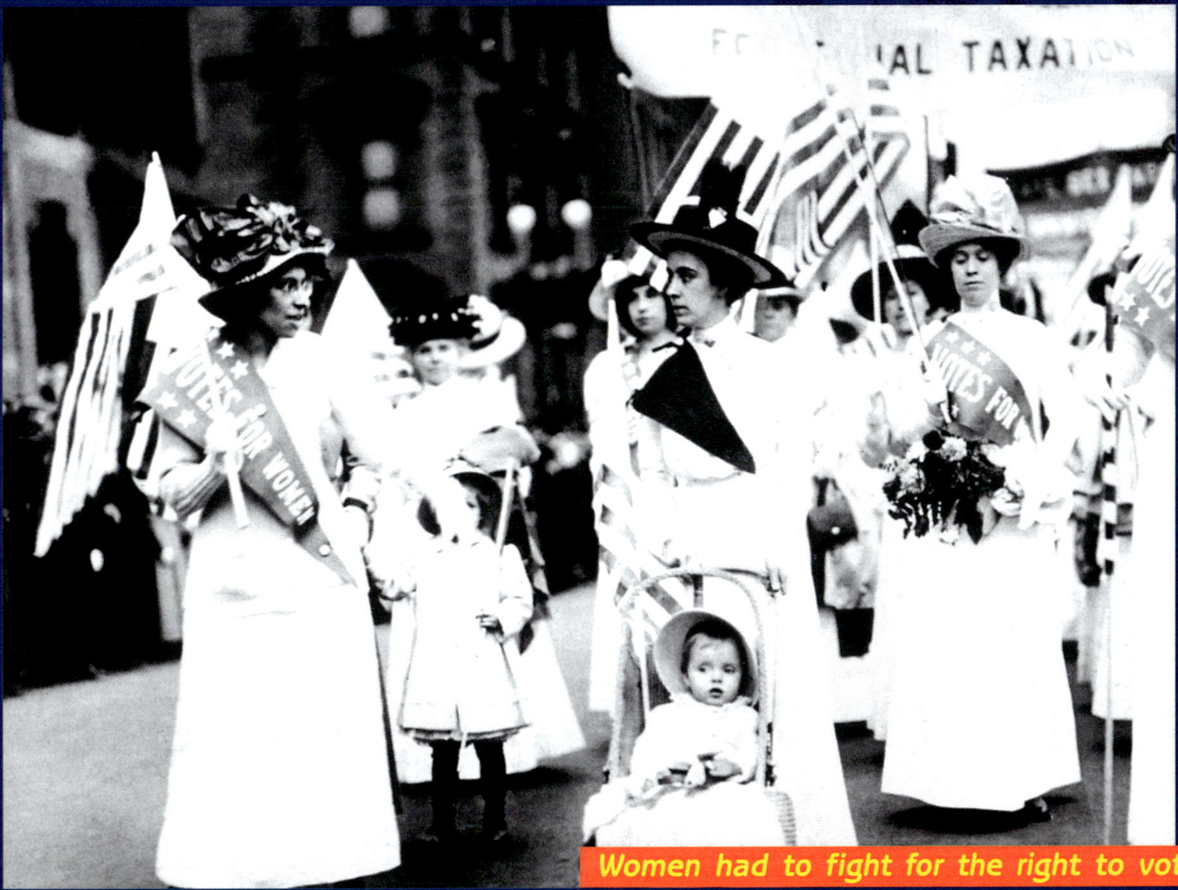

Women had to fight for the right to vote.

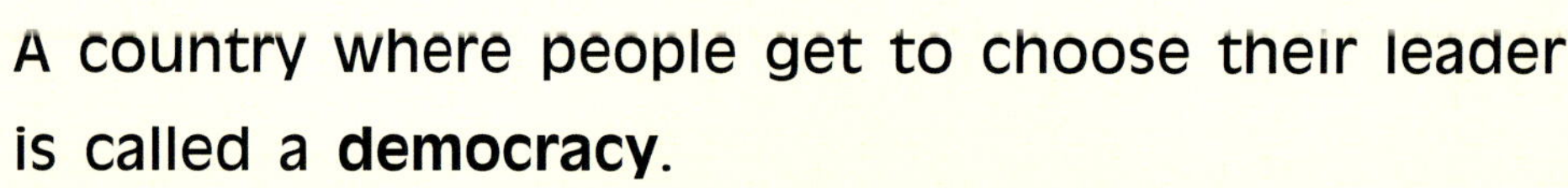

A country where people get to choose their leader is called a **democracy**.

In a democracy, all adults have the right to vote.

Here are some countries that have a democracy.

Many people think that voting is the most important right people have.

Glossary

democracy a country where people get to vote for the leaders they want

secret ballot when people can vote without others knowing who or what they voted for

Index